P9-AON-877

Level E

Reading Explorations

Globe Fearon

Writers: Joanne Suter and Sandra Widener
Senior Editor: Nance Davidson
Project Editors: Marion Castellucci, Amy Jolin,
    Robert McIlwaine
Editorial Assistant: Marilyn Bashoff
Production Editor: Rosann Bar
Electronic Page Production: Heather Roake
Electronic Art: Armando Baez

Printed in the United States of America
1 2 3 4 5 6 7 8 9 10   99 98 97 96 95

ISBN 0-835-93444-6

Globe Fearon Educational Publisher
A Division of Simon & Schuster
Upper Saddle River, New Jersey

Contents

Social Studies

In these stories you will read about the destruction of a great city and the sinking of a great ship. You will also read about the two world wars.

The 1906 Earthquake

WORDS TO KNOW

San Francisco (san fran-SIHS-koh) a big city in California

earthquake (ERTH-kwayk) a shaking movement of the earth

damage (DAM-ihj) harm that makes something have less value

dynamite (DEYE-nuh-meyet) the material used to blow something up

debris (duh-BREE) the remains of things that have been destroyed

Once in a while, something happens that changes many lives. In 1906, the lives of the people of **San Francisco** were changed in a minute.

The date was April 18, 1906. It was very early in the morning. San Francisco was very quiet. Some bakers were just opening their shops. But most people were still home in bed.

Then, at 5:12 A.M., the ground began to shake hard. The **earthquake** lasted for a little more than a minute. When it was over, much of the city had been destroyed.

The huge earthquake did great **damage**. It ripped apart brick buildings. It broke wooden houses into splinters. It pulled pipes and steel rails from the ground. It made bridges crack and fall. Many people were hurt. In one long minute, the earthquake changed many lives.

When the shaking stopped, people came out into the streets. Many were shocked at what they saw. Soon, they heard cries for help. People trapped in fallen buildings were calling out. Those outside tried to rescue them.

Then people noticed the smoke. Fires were breaking out all over the city. The earthquake had ripped out electrical wires. It had caused gas pipes to explode. Stoves and gas lamps had been knocked over. To make things worse, the city's fire alarms were not working. The earthquake had destroyed them, too.

Still, firefighters did their best. All over the city, they hitched horses to the fire wagons. They got to many of the fires. They attached their hoses to fire hydrants. No water came out! Most of the city's water pipes were broken. With no water to stop them, the fires spread quickly.

1. What damage did the earthquake do?

2. How do you think the shaking earth could do so much damage?

The police and the army tried another way to stop the fires. They used **dynamite**. They blew up buildings close to the fires. Where buildings once stood, there were big spaces. They hoped these spaces would stop the fires from spreading. The plan didn't work very well.

The fires burned for three days. Finally, most of the fires just burned out. They burned until there was nothing left to burn.

The city was in ruins. City hall was destroyed. Hotels, libraries, restaurants, and theaters were gone. Dozens of churches and schools were in ashes. The whole downtown area was destroyed. More than 250,000 homes were lost.

Homeless people walked the streets. They carried what they owned with them. Many people went up into the hills.

City workers got busy right away. They tried to get help for the city and its people. People without homes needed places to stay. Injured people needed care. Almost everyone needed food and water.

News in the city was hard to come by. Newspaper offices were destroyed. The phones did not work. People only knew what they heard from each other.

News of the earthquake spread quickly outside the city. Many other cities sent help. Trains came from around the country. They carried food, clothes, and other needed things. Congress voted to give the city $2.5 million. Money also came from many other countries.

At first, life was very hard. The army put up tent camps for the homeless. People camped out in the parks. Some people still had their homes. But they were afraid to return. They thought an earthquake might hit again.

Little by little, the people of the city cleaned up. It was a big job. They used picks and shovels. They loaded the **debris** on wagons. Horses took the loaded wagons away to the dump outside the city.

People began to rebuild. By the end of May, almost everyone had running water. Electricity was back by June. The biggest job was replacing all the destroyed buildings. That took much longer.

Still, within three years a lot had been done. About 20,000 buildings had been replaced. The people of San Francisco had done a great job. The city was on its way back.

For some, life returned to normal. For others, life would never be the same. They would always remember 5:12 A.M. on April 18, 1906. It was the longest minute of their lives.

3. What caused the most damage to the city?

4. What were some problems that the firefighters faced after the earthquake?

5. What was the most important thing to be done right after the earthquake? Why?

6. Why do you think people help others in places far away when something bad happens?

The Titanic

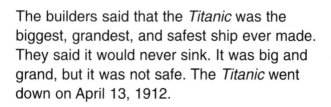

WORDS TO KNOW

watertight (WAW-tuhr-teyet) made so that water cannot get in or out

icebergs (EYES-bergz) big mountains of ice that float in the ocean

crew (kroo) the people who sail a ship

lifeboats (LEYEF-bohtz) small boats carried by a large ship. They are used to save people if the ship sinks.

The builders said that the *Titanic* was the biggest, grandest, and safest ship ever made. They said it would never sink. It was big and grand, but it was not safe. The *Titanic* went down on April 13, 1912.

On April 10, 1912, a ship whistle blew. The people on the ship waved to those on the dock. The huge ship began to move. Slowly, the *Titanic* sailed away from Great Britain, an island country in Europe. It headed for New York.

The *Titanic* was a great, new ship. It was the biggest ship ever built. It was as long as three football fields. The cabins where people slept were like fine hotel rooms. The dining room was the grandest ever built. Hundreds of people could eat at the same time.

The *Titanic* also was built for safety. The builders had made many **watertight** sections. Water could not leak from one section to another. If one section flooded, it could be closed off. Then water would not get into the other sections. The ship would not fill up with water. The builders said it was the first ship that could not sink.

This trip from Great Britain to New York was the first voyage of the *Titanic*. At that time, there was only one way to cross the ocean: by ship. The *Titanic* was the grandest one ever built. Many people wanted to be on its first trip.

1. Today we cross the ocean by plane. In 1912, how did people cross?

2. Where was the *Titanic* going on its first trip?

All the cabins on the *Titanic* were full for this trip. There were about 2,200 people on board. Many were rich and famous. Some were crossing the ocean to visit family and friends. Still others had business in the United States. The *Titanic* was the best ship to take!

The first few days of the voyage went smoothly. There were parties every day and night. All the people were having a wonderful time. By the evening of the fourth day, the ship was more than halfway across the Atlantic Ocean. It was traveling in icy water. In two days it would reach New York.

There were other ships in the area. They knew that the Atlantic Ocean was dangerous.

They had seen huge **icebergs** near the *Titanic*. Some icebergs were so big that they could sink any ship. The other ships in the area sent radio messages to the *Titanic* about the icebergs. But no one on the *Titanic* saw any. It was late at night and very dark. Most people were asleep.

Then all of a sudden, the **crew** saw something. It rose up before them. It was as high as the ship.

Quickly, the crew tried to turn the ship away. They shut off the engines to slow the ship down. They turned the wheel as far as it would go. But it was too late. The iceberg scraped the ship below the water.

At first, no one was worried. "After all," they thought, "this ship could not sink."

But the iceberg had cut the bottom of the ship. Water poured into many sections. It was coming in fast. Water was filling each section and spilling over into the next. Soon many of the lower sections of the ship were full. The crew knew that the *Titanic* was going to sink.

They rushed to the ship's radio. They called

other ships for help. One ship said it would hurry, but it was far away. Another ship was very close. The people on the *Titanic* could even see it. But that ship did not answer the call for help. The *Titanic* shot lights into the sky. Still, the ship did not answer.

The *Titanic* was filling with water. People were coming up out of their flooding cabins onto the decks. The crew got the **lifeboats** ready. They lowered these small boats into the water when some were only half full. Even worse, there were not enough boats for everyone. Only half the people could fit into the lifeboats. The other half would not be able to get off the ship.

The people in the lifeboats watched the *Titanic*. The lights in the ship went out. One end of the ship rose up out of the water. The great ship slid under the ocean.

Of the 2,200 people on the ship, 1,503 died. A rescue ship picked up the people in lifeboats.

The *Titanic* never finished its first trip. The ship that could not sink went under the ocean in less than 3 hours.

After the *Titanic* sank, many ships became safer. Builders had to put enough lifeboats to carry all the people on each ship they built. Also, special ships were sent out just to watch for icebergs and warn other ships. These things did not help the people who died when the *Titanic* sank. But they did help those who crossed the ocean in later years.

3. What did the *Titanic* hit that made it sink?

4. Why do you think the ship's builders had not put enough lifeboats on the *Titanic*?

5. Why do you think some of the lifeboats were put into the water before they were completely full?

6. Why do you think people made ships safer after the *Titanic* went down?

Weapons of World War I

In all areas of life, people find new ways to do things. During World War I, people tried new ways to win battles.

In 1914, the world saw a new kind of war. Many, many countries fought in this war. So many countries fought that it was called a *world* war. Today, we call it World War I, or the first World War.

World War I was different from other wars. One reason was the number of countries that fought. There were 15. On one side of the fight, the most important country was **Germany**. On the other side, the most important countries were **France** and Great Britain. In 1917, the United States joined France and Great Britain to fight against Germany.

Before 1914, most wars were fought on giant battlefields. Armies from each side lined up. They pointed their guns. Then soldiers ran toward each other, firing their guns.

In World War I, battlefields changed. Armies from both sides dug giant **trenches**. They were long, deep holes in the ground. Soldiers could stand in them. They could also walk a long way in the trenches. Soldiers placed mounds of dirt and wire fences all around the trenches. This helped protect them.

The soldiers climbed into the trenches. Then they fired their guns at the enemy across the battlefield. Of course, the enemy had dug its own trenches. The soldiers on the other side were fighting the same way.

The trenches brought new dangers, though. Sometimes enemy bombs and shells hit a trench. Mounds of dirt flew everywhere. Men were buried alive.

Also, the soldiers began to get sick. Many men had to stand close together for days and weeks. When it rained, the trenches filled with water and mud. Soon, many soldiers were very ill. Millions of men died in the trenches. They died from bombs, guns, and sickness.

1. List the most important countries that fought in World War I.

2. How did trenches protect soldiers?

3. How did the trenches harm soldiers?

There were other reasons the war was different. The enemies began to use new **weapons** in World War I.

In 1915, Germany began using **poison gas**. This gas could not be seen. It burned the skin and eyes. It hurt the lungs. The poison gas caused great pain. It sometimes caused death. The only protection was a gas mask. France and Great Britain saw how the gas was used. Soon, they began using it too.

Great Britain developed tanks for war on land. These huge rolling vehicles drove across battlefields firing their guns. Enemy bullets bounced off the metal sides of the tanks. Soldiers of Germany were frightened by these "iron monsters."

Germany built a deadly new kind of ship. These ships were called **submarines**. From under water, submarines could sneak up on other ships. Submarines sank many ships.

Both sides in the war fought battles in the air. Airplanes had only been around for a few years. But both Germany and Great Britain saw how they could be used. They put machine guns and bombs on them. They attacked each other's factories and train stations. They even bombed cities. Now the war could be fought from the sky.

From 1914 to 1918, countries found many new ways of making war. They dug trenches. They used poison gas, submarines, and tanks. They fought with airplanes. When it was all over, many people were dead. More people died in World War I than in any war before. More than 8 million people had died. Another 20 million were wounded. The new weapons had worked all too well. They changed the way wars are fought.

4. Why was poison gas dangerous?

5. Why was it important that submarines could sneak up on other ships?

6. How were airplanes used during the war?

7. Why do you think countries still make new kinds of weapons?

D-Day

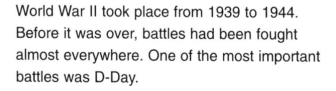

WORDS TO KNOW

invade (ihn-VAYD) to enter by force

Adolf Hitler (AH-dahlf HIHT-luhr) the ruler of Germany from 1933 to 1945

Allies (AL-eyez) the countries that fought against Germany in World War II

Axis powers (AK-sihs POW-uhrz) the countries that fought against the Allies in World War II

Italy (IHT-uhl-ee) a country in Europe

Japan (juh-PAN) a country in the Pacific Ocean

World War II took place from 1939 to 1944. Before it was over, battles had been fought almost everywhere. One of the most important battles was D-Day.

On June 6, 1944, thousands of soldiers set sail from Great Britain in hundreds of boats. They were mostly soldiers of the United States and Great Britain. That day the soldiers landed in France. They were going to **invade** Europe to take it back from Germany. D-Day, as it was called, was one of the most important days of World War II.

World War II began in 1939 when Germany took over many countries in Europe. At that time, Germany was led by **Adolf Hitler**. Hitler thought Germany should rule the world. He started by taking over almost all of Europe. By 1940, only two countries had not been taken over. One was Great Britain in the west. The other was the Soviet Union in the east. The Soviet Union was a large country in both Asia and Europe. Together, Great Britain and the Soviet Union were called the **Allies**.

The Germans attacked Great Britain for a long time. They bombed its cities every night. They attacked its ships. They killed many people, but Great Britain did not give up.

Europe in World War II 1939-1944

N
W E
S

GREAT BRITAIN

D-Day Landing

ATLANTIC OCEAN

FRANCE

GERMANY

GERMANY

SOVIET UNION

ITALY

Mediterranean Sea

KEY
■ Axis Powers
■ Countries taken over by Axis Powers
▨ Allied Powers
□ Countries not in the War

In 1941, Germany invaded the Soviet Union. For a time, it looked like Germany would win. But the people of the Soviet Union fought back. Soon, Hitler was fighting the war on two sides. He was fighting Great Britain in the west and the Soviet Union in the east.

That year the United States joined the war on the Allies' side. Along with Great Britain and the Soviet Union, the United States fought the **Axis** powers. The Axis countries were Germany, **Italy**, and **Japan**.

1. Which countries of Europe fought Germany in the east and west?

2. Name two of the Allies.

3. Name two of the Axis powers.

The war went on. There were battles in almost all parts of the world. The Axis powers wanted to control the world. The Allies tried to hold them back. They tried to free the countries that had been taken over by the Axis powers.

By 1944, one thing was becoming clear. The Allies were going to win. Germany had lost thousands of troops. Soldiers were short of supplies. But Hitler was not ready to give up. Germany still held most of Europe.

The Allies knew that to win they had to take back Europe. It would not be easy. Hitler had built strong defenses. There were forts, tanks, and big guns along the shores of the Atlantic Ocean. Hitler called these defenses the Atlantic Wall. To take back Europe, the Allies would have to cross the Atlantic Wall.

The Allies knew of Hitler's Atlantic Wall. They had plans of their own. They would not go ashore at regular landing places. They would use special boats to land soldiers on beaches in France.

The Allies had a million troops ready to fight. Some would be in the first group to land in France. Others would follow with supplies. Still others would help the soldiers in France from the sea and from the air.

At 2 A.M. on June 6, 1944, D-Day began. The Allies headed for a beach in France. At 6:30 A.M., the first soldiers and tanks went ashore. The German army fought back. The fighting was very heavy. Thousands died that day on both sides.

All over the world, people waited for news. In the United States, life almost stopped. Stores and shops closed. Church bells rang. People streamed out into the streets.

Slowly, the news came. The Allies had landed.

Fighting was heavy. But the Allies were pushing the army of Germany back. The Atlantic Wall was crumbling. The Allies were winning!

D-Day was a success. But World War II did not end that day. Almost a year passed before the Allies reached Germany. Finally, the war ended in August 1945. Today, D-Day is remembered as the day the Allies started to win the war.

4. Why were Germany's defenses along the coast called the Atlantic Wall?

5. Why was D-Day so important?

6. Why didn't World War II end with D-Day?

7. Why do you think this war was called a "world war"?

Science

In these pages you'll read
about two things that make
you special—your fingerprints
and your genes. You'll also
explore space.

Fingerprints

Here is a riddle. What is something you always have with you? These things never change. They always look the same. No one else in the world has the same ones you do. The answer is your fingerprints.

It's a fact. No two people in the whole world have the same fingerprints. Even twins have different ones.

Fingerprints are **patterns**. These designs are formed by lines that cover the skin of your fingertips. You can see these lines. Look closely at your fingertips. There are wavy lines on each finger. Those are your fingerprints.

People who study fingerprints have grouped them. There are three main patterns. One is the *loop pattern*. It is the most common. The lines begin on one side of the finger. They curve back sharply. Then they end on the same side.

Another kind is a *whorl pattern*. The lines form a circle. The third is called an *arch pattern*. The lines reach from one side of the finger to the other. They rise in the center. There are many fingerprints with no set form. This is called the *accidental pattern*. It can be made of loops, whorls, and arches.

Arch Pattern

Loop Pattern

Whorl Pattern

There are three main groups of fingerprints. Many fingerprints are made up of all three groups.

Fingerprints usually stay the same all your life. The only way they change is if you have a disease or an accident or if your fingers are burned.

1. Name one pattern of fingerprints and tell what it looks like.

2. Look at one of your fingers. Which pattern does it look like the most?

Fingerprints are very important. They are used to **identify** people. They can tell us who a person is. To do this, a copy has to be made of the fingerprints. A special ink is placed on a piece of glass or metal. The fingertips are pressed into the ink. They are rolled from one side to the other. The fingers are then pressed on a white card. Now the fingerprints can be seen.

Police use fingerprints a lot. They call them "prints." Many **criminals**, or people who break the law, leave their prints behind. Sometimes the prints can be seen easily. This happens when criminals with blood or dirt on their fingers touch something. The police take a picture of the fingerprints. They compare them to the prints of the criminals they know. If they match, the police have found someone who might have done the crime.

Sometimes the fingerprints on an object have been made by the oil and sweat on a person's hand. They are not **visible**. Even though they can't be seen, they are there. To be used, these prints must be made visible.

There are two ways to do this. One way is used on hard things, such as metal and wood. A colored powder is brushed on. The powder sticks to the oil in the prints. A sticky tape is pressed against the powder. The prints come off onto the tape. Then the police take a picture of the tape.

The other way is used on soft things, such as paper or cloth. Chemicals are used on soft things. They mix with the sweat from the print. The chemicals make the print show up. A picture is taken of the print.

Fingerprints are used by more people than the police. Some businesses use them. They take fingerprints of new workers. They have the fingerprints checked on computers. They check to see if the prints match those of any known criminals. The army and government offices use fingerprints this way, too.

Fingerprints are also used to help identify people who die. People who die in airplane crashes or fires may be hard to identify just by looking. But their fingerprints can still be taken and matched.

There is an old saying: "Your fingerprints are your **signature**." Signing your name is something only you can do. Although people have faked another person's signature, no one can fake your fingerprints.

3. Explain two ways to make fingerprints visible.

4. What kind of businesses do you think might use fingerprints to check on new workers?

5. Why are fingerprints important?

Genes and Environment

You may be a lot like your mother and father. But you are also special. Read this to find out why this is true.

You may have known two sisters who didn't look anything alike. Maybe one sister was tall with straight brown hair and dark eyes. The other was short with curly black hair and blue eyes. They both had the same parents. Yet, they didn't even look as if they came from the same family!

The reason this can happen is in their **genes.** Genes are tiny structures inside the body's cells. They control the thousands of **physical traits** that people get from their parents. For example, they control the color of a person's hair and eyes. They control whether someone will be tall or short.

Genes come in pairs. Half your genes come from your mother. The other half comes from your father. That's why you may look like one or both of your parents. But you are not an exact copy of either of them. Genes can combine in different ways in children with the same parents. That's why brothers and sisters sometimes don't look like each other.

Each gene carries specific information. For example, there is a gene for eye color. A child gets one eye-color gene from each parent. The combination of the two genes controls the color of the child's eyes. One combination of genes will make blue eyes. Another one will make brown eyes.

1. What are genes?

2. What is a physical trait?

3. Give an example of a physical trait.

Genes control many physical traits passed from parents to children. Not all traits are physical, though. We have **personality traits**, too. Some people are talkative. Others are quiet. Some people are careful. Others are careless. These traits can come from parents. But they can also be learned from outside things. A person's **environment** can form them.

Sometimes environment can even affect a trait from a parent. For example, a child may get a talent for music from a parent. A talent is a natural ability to do something well. But in order to be a good musician, the child has to take lessons and practice. That is part of the child's environment.

The genes you have control a lot about the way you look, feel, and behave. But genes are not the only things that affect you. There are outside things, too. There are the friends you make. There are the books you read. And there are the things you learn and like to do.

All these things make you the person that you are. Each person is a special mix of genes and environment.

4. What are personality traits?

5. How can the environment affect personality traits?

6. What physical traits did you get from your parents?

7. What personality traits did you learn from your environment?

Sputnik

The United States worked very hard to beat the Soviets in the race for space. But the first winner was the Soviet Union.

On October 4, 1957, a **rocket** sent a **satellite** into space. It wasn't very big. It was only 23 inches wide. It weighed only 184 pounds. Yet it was much more important than its size. It caused the start of a race. The race was called "the space race."

The little satellite was called *Sputnik*. It was the first thing ever sent into outer space. The country that launched it was the Soviet Union.

In the 1950s, the Soviet Union and the United States were not friendly. Their governments were very different. They disagreed over many things.

The two countries competed in many ways. One way was in **technology**. When it came to machines, the United States had always been the best. It made the best cars and planes. It made better machines of almost every kind.

The United States was shocked when the Soviets made *Sputnik*. The Soviets had sent a satellite into space first. The satellite was a great machine. This meant that the Soviets were the best in space technology. The space race had begun. The United States was left at the starting line.

1. What was the first thing ever sent into space?

2. Who was winning the space race in 1957? Tell why.

Not everyone was upset by *Sputnik*, though. Many people around the world were excited. People interested in outer space were thrilled. They did not care who had made *Sputnik*.

Sputnik stayed in space for several weeks. It traveled in an **orbit**. It went around Earth. One orbit took 96 minutes. Its highest point above Earth was 585 miles. From Earth, *Sputnik* looked like a shooting star streaking across the sky. Finally, *Sputnik* fell out of orbit and burned up in the air.

In November 1957, the Soviet Union launched *Sputnik II*. It carried a dog named Laika. Laika was the first living thing to orbit Earth. *Sputnik II* stayed in space for 6 months.

The Soviets launched eight more satellites. They also carried animals into space. Many tests and studies were done on these trips. The animals were tested to see how they did in space. The satellites sent back information about Earth.

Finally, in February 1958, the United States launched its first satellite. It was called *Explorer I*. It was smaller than *Sputnik*. But it went much higher. It went 1,600 miles above Earth. Then the United States launched *Vanguard I*. This satellite orbited Earth. It sent back important information.

Still, the United States was worried. The Soviets were still winning the space race. Some Americans were afraid of what the Soviets might do. They might find a way to put bombs on their rockets. They would be able to drop bombs on the United States from space.

In 1958, the United States set up NASA. It stands for **N**ational **A**eronautic and **S**pace **A**dministration. NASA was the group in charge of the U.S. space program. Its job was to design, build, and launch rockets for exploring space. One day, people would be sent into orbit. People would be sent to the moon. Both the Soviet Union and the United States wanted to be the first to do these things.

In the late 1950s, the United States was still in second place. The Soviet Union had taken a big first step. It had changed the world forever with a small object named *Sputnik*.

3. How were *Sputnik* and *Explorer I* similar? How were they different?

4. Why do you think animals were sent into space before people were?

5. Why do you think the United States and the Soviet Union were in a space race?

6. What was NASA's job?

7. Why do you think the United States was shocked by *Sputnik?*

Going to Mars

Mars is one of our closest neighbors in space. Still, it is millions of miles away. Someday, people may travel to Mars. They may even live on the planet.

Imagine yourself in about 40 years. It's the year 2040. You and billions of other people are watching TV. You're looking at two **astronauts** getting out of a **spacecraft**. Your parents are watching with you. They're smiling. They remember watching a scene like this when they were children. In 1969, they watched two astronauts land on the moon, 240,000 miles from Earth.

This time the event is even more incredible. The astronauts are about to land *millions* of miles away. They're about to set foot on the planet Mars!

This may sound impossible to you. People said landing on the moon was impossible, yet it happened. It may be possible to land on Mars someday, too.

People have always wanted to go to Mars. That's easy to understand. Mars is about the same size as Earth. It has many of the same features. Its day is about as long as a day on Earth. The temperature on most of the planet is about the same, too. In fact, the red planet Mars has been called Earth's "red twin."

1. Which is farther away, Mars or the moon?

2. Name two ways Mars is like Earth.

We first learned a lot about Mars in the 1960s. A spacecraft flew within 6,000 miles of the planet. Its machines sent back many pictures. It sent back information about Mars's weather and thin air. It told scientists many things they did not know.

In 1976, two spacecraft landed on Mars. Machines sent back information about the soil and rocks. This information gave hints that once there was some form of life on Mars.

During the 1980s and 1990s, scientists learned more about Mars from studying **meteorites**. These objects had broken loose from the planet's crust. They traveled through space and landed on Earth thousands of years ago. One meteorite showed the clearest sign yet that life could have existed on Mars.

That meteorite caused great excitement. In it, scientists found what they think was left of a form of life that once lived on Mars.

These **organisms** would have been tiny. They are the first sign that life may have existed anyplace else than on Earth.

These signs of life are billions of years old. Space scientists want to know if life really existed on Mars. They also want to know why it disappeared. They want to go to Mars to find out.

There is another reason space scientists want to go to Mars. They think that someday humans may be able to live there. But that day is a long way off. Before it can happen, we have to learn much more about the planet.

The next big step for exploring Mars is to send a spacecraft there to collect things. A spaceship would orbit the planet. It would send a landing spacecraft down to Mars.

This spacecraft would move across the planet's surface. It would use robot arms to gather rocks and soil. Then it would return to the spaceship for the trip back to Earth. Back on Earth, scientists would study the rocks and soil.

Sending a spacecraft to collect things from

Mars is still a few years away. Scientists hope to launch such a spacecraft by 2003. Until then, other spacecraft will be sent to Mars. They will land in different areas of the planet. They will send back pictures. They will send back maps of the surface. They will measure the air. They also will dig into the soil and study it. They will send all this information back to Earth.

Sending people to Mars is probably many years away. That trip will be very difficult. Mars is millions of miles from Earth. It will take months just to get there. The astronauts will be in space for a very long time. That may cause them to have health problems.

There are other problems. A spacecraft carrying people to Mars would need a great deal of fuel. It would have to be very heavy. It would also cost a lot of money to build.

Astronauts also have to plan for staying alive on Mars. There is no food or water. Astronauts would have to bring what they need with them.

All these problems will be hard to solve. A human being might never be able to land on Mars. Still, space scientists have hope. After all, 50 years ago no one even dreamed we could send someone to the moon.

One thing is for sure. We will continue to explore Mars with more spacecraft. The more we learn about Mars, the more we want to know. That's why this planet is the next great step into space.

3. What have meteorites shown us about Mars?

4. Why do you think people would want to live on Mars?

5. Why will sending a human being to Mars be so hard?

6. Do you think traveling to Mars is important? Why or why not?

Math

Money is the subject of three stories in this section. The last story will tell you how the odds can either be for or against you.

Gross Domestic Product

Each country produces **goods** and **services.** If you know how much a country produces each year, you will know how well or how poorly the people in the country live.

One way to know how well a country is doing is to find its Gross Domestic Product. This is the total cost of all the goods and services made in a country in one year. Gross Domestic Product is called GDP for short.

Here's how people figure out a country's GDP. First, they find out what goods are made in the country. Goods are things like corn, milk, silver rings, clothing, and boats. People find the cost of all the things made in the country. Then they add those costs to get the **value** of all the goods.

Next, they find out the services people do. Services are tasks done for others, such as teaching children or raking lawns. Then they find out how much money all these services are worth. They add these amounts to find the value of all the services.

Finally, they add the cost of the goods to the cost of the services. The total is the Gross Domestic Product. In **Hungary**, the GDP is $55.4 billion. In **India**, the GDP is $240 billion. In **South Africa**, the GDP is $81 billion.

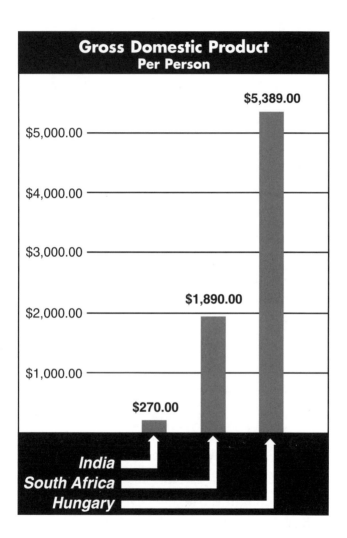

Gross Domestic Product
Per Person

1. What is the Gross Domestic Product of a country?

2. Which has the largest GDP, Hungary, India, or South Africa?

It may seem like India has more money than Hungary and South Africa. India has the largest GDP. But India also has many more people than Hungary and South Africa. India must provide for more people with its GDP. The people in India do not have more money than people in Hungary or South Africa.

To find out more about each country, divide the GDP by the number of people in the country. That will tell more about how much money the people in the country have. It will tell you the per person GDP.

Hungary has 10,300,000 people. When you divide its GDP by this number, you find that for each person in Hungary, the GDP is $5,380. That means that an average person in Hungary can live on $5,380 for one year. Of course, some people have much more money than the per person GDP. Some people have much less money. The per person GDP only tells the average amount of money per person.

South Africa has 39,550,000 people. The GDP for each person is $1,890. India has 911,600,000 people. Its per person GDP is $270. This shows that India is actually poor. Its total GDP is large, but many people live there. The GDP for each person is small.

There are many reasons why a country has a low GDP. Maybe many people are out of work. Maybe a country has very few resources. A country's GDP will be higher when the people produce more goods and services. When a country's GDP is higher, there will be more money in the country for the people.

3. How do you find the per person GDP?

4. What does the per person GDP tell about the people in a country?

5. How can India create a higher GDP?

The Price of Shoes

How much did your last pair of shoes cost?
They probably cost a lot. Here is what you are
really paying for when you buy a pair of shoes.

When Howard paid $50 for a new pair of shoes, he wondered why a bit of leather, rubber, and plastic cost so much. These **raw materials**, or basic things used to make products, can't cost that much money.

It's not that simple, of course. Even if Howard had the leather, rubber, and plastic, he couldn't make a pair of running shoes by himself. When people buy shoes, they are buying much more than the materials. Here's a look at what the money is really paying for.

Let's say Dan owns a shoe company. He is proud of making shoes that are very well suited for different sports. The tennis shoes are different from the basketball shoes. The running shoes are different, too. Each type of shoe has been carefully made by Dan's company.

Dan has paid for **research and development** on his shoes. First he does research about the human foot. He studies what the foot does during each sport. For example, the movements during tennis are quite different from those made when someone runs.

Once Dan understands what the foot does during a sport, he designs a shoe that will help the foot's movements. Dan might make a few kinds of each shoe. Then he has runners test them to see what works best. Finally, after many changes, Dan chooses the best running shoes. The company thinks runners will buy these shoes.

All this research and development costs money. Research and development costs are what a company spends to create its product.

1. What are raw materials?

2. What costs does a company have when it is creating a product?

Research and development for this running shoe cost many thousands of dollars. Dan's company will be making many thousands of pairs of these running shoes. So the cost is spread out over all the pairs. For one pair of running shoes, these costs may be about $1. For another type of shoe, the research and development costs might be more or less.

Next, Dan's company buys raw materials. The company's buyers shop for leather, rubber, plastic, and cloth. To get the lowest prices, they shop all over the world. They also buy many pounds of each material to save money. Dan's company spends many thousands of dollars. For each pair of shoes, the company might spend $4 on raw materials.

Dan also has to pay for the costs of running his business. All the people who work there must be paid. These costs are all part of each pair of shoes, too. Dan divides these costs among all the shoes he makes. For each pair of running shoes, Dan might add $4.50 for the cost of running his business.

Now Dan has a great pair of shoes. But without advertising, no one will know about them. Dan pays to have commercials and ads made. Advertising adds about $0.50 to Dan's cost for each pair of shoes.

The shoes cost Dan $10 to research, develop, and sell. But Dan doesn't sell them for $10. Dan sells them to a shoe store for $20.

That is $10 more than it cost Dan's company to make the shoes. Dan has a $10 **profit** on each pair of shoes.

Lisa owns a shoe store. She has bought Dan's shoes for $20. She is not going to sell them for $20, though. Lisa has other costs. She pays to run the store. She pays sales people to sell the shoes. She pays for more advertising, too. People need to know that they can buy these running shoes at Lisa's store.

All those costs add about $6 to the cost of each pair of shoes. Each pair of shoes costs Lisa $26 now. But Lisa is not going to sell the shoes for $26. She needs to make a profit, too. She sells the shoes for $50. That will give her a profit of $24.

Finally, Howard buys the running shoes at Lisa's store. At $50, everyone has made money along the way. Howard's $50 has paid for a lot. With any luck, the shoes will be wonderful. Howard will be happy even though he has spent a lot of money.

3. What costs does the shoe company have?

4. How are the costs of the shoe company and the shoe store the same?

5. Why do you think advertising is important for both the shoe company and the shoe store?

6. Why is the cost of materials such a small part of the cost of the shoes?

Interest

WORDS TO KNOW

savings account (SAY-vingz uh-KOWNT)
a place to keep money. Savings accounts
are arranged by banks.

interest (IHN-trihst) money paid for the use
of money

compound interest (CAHM-pownd IHN-trihst)
money earned on the original money plus
the interest already earned

Let's say you have some extra money. You
have a choice of where to save it. You could
keep it under your mattress or in a bank. Does
it really matter? Read this article and find out.

Fred has $100 he wants to save. Juana has $100 to save, too. Here's what each of them did with their money. Their choices made a big difference in how much money each had after 10 years.

Fred decided to put his money into a **savings account** at Grand Bank. The bank pays **interest** of 4 percent a year on the money in savings accounts. The interest is the money the bank will pay Fred for keeping his money there. For the first year that Fred's $100 is in the account, he will get $4 interest. At the end of the year, Fred will have $104 in his savings account.

Juana decides to put her money in a savings account at State Bank. This bank pays 6 percent interest a year. For the first year that Juana has $100 in the savings account, she will earn $6. At the end of the year, Juana will have $106 in the account.

1. What is interest?

2. Why does Juana earn more interest than Fred?

There is not much difference in the interest Fred and Juana earn in the first year. Fred gets $4, and Juana gets $6. That $2 difference may not seem like much.

However, as each year passes, the difference in what they earn on their money will grow. The reason is **compound interest**. Compound interest is the money a bank pays not just on the money that Fred or Juana started with, but also on the interest they already earned.

For example, during the second year Fred will get 4 percent interest, not on the $100 he started with but on the $104 now in the account. Fred will have $108.16 at the end of the year. Juana will get 6 percent interest on $106, not $100. Juana will have $112.36 at the end of the second year. At the end of the third year, Fred will have saved $112.48. Juana will have saved $119.10.

By the end of five years, Fred's $100 is worth $121.67. Juana's $100 is worth $133.82.

By the end of 10 years, the difference is even greater. Fred's $100 is worth $148.02.

Juana's $100 is worth $179.08. Juana has made $31.06 more on her money. Also, Juana's $100 has grown to $179.08 without any work at all. The decision she made 10 years earlier is really paying off.

3. How does compound interest work?

4. Why does compound interest make such a difference in the money the two accounts earned in 10 years?

5. Why would Fred and Juana earn less money over 10 years if they took out the interest each year?

Against the Odds

Raymond is sure he doesn't have to worry about doing well in school. He's going to play professional basketball. His friend Alonzo thinks he's crazy to count on that. Find out why.

"Hey, Raymond, did you finish the book report yet?" Alonzo asked. Raymond and Alonzo were shooting hoops.

"No," Raymond said, taking a shot. "I'm not worrying about school anymore."

"You're kidding," Alonzo said. "What are you going to do, drop out?"

"No. I'm going to get a scholarship, go to college, and then play pro ball."

"Are you crazy?" Alonzo asked. "You can't count on that. I read somewhere that the **odds** are against anyone going on to play professional basketball."

"I will," Raymond said, taking another shot. "The coach thinks I'm really good. Besides, the pro teams need new players every year."

"I bet you'll be surprised exactly how few players make it," Alonzo said.

"Surprise me, then," Raymond said.

Alonzo did some research. In two weeks, he was back. "Hey, Raymond. You want to hear about the pros?"

"Sure," Raymond said.

"OK. Listen to this," Alonzo said. "There are 154,000 seniors playing high school basketball. There are only 4,000 places for high school seniors on college teams. Only 2.6 **percent** of seniors even make the team when they get to college. That means that not even 3 seniors out of every 100 make the team."

1. What percent of high school seniors play basketball when they get to college?

2. Why does Alonzo tell Raymond he should not count on playing pro ball?

"I'm the best we've got," Raymond said. "I've got scouts watching me now."

"Okay," Alonzo said. "Let's say you make a college team. By the time college players are in their last year of college, there are about 2,800 of them playing. Want to guess how many go on to the pros?"

"Let me think," Raymond said. "Six hundred?"

"Wrong. Only about 50," Alonzo said. "Listen to this. It's from the information the college people sent me. Only 1.8 percent of college seniors play at least one year in pro basketball. Out of every 100 players, there aren't even 2 who get to the pros."

"Fifty? In all of pro basketball? That can't be right," Raymond said.

"Yeah, it's right. Fifty new players a year. It's pretty depressing."

"So what are you saying?"

"I'm saying we can all have fun shooting hoops. And you know you're a great player. Maybe you'll get lucky. But with those odds, you'd better finish your book report."

3. How many new professional basketball players are there every year?

4. What percent of college players go on to play professional basketball?

5. Why is Alonzo trying to talk Raymond into finishing his book report?

Life Skills

You'll learn why smart shopping and breakfast are important. You'll read about exercise and about calling for help when you need it.

Smart Shopper

WORDS TO KNOW

coupons (KOO-pahnz) special slips of paper that allow you to save money when you buy something

circular (SER-kyuh-luhr) the paper that a store prints each week to tell what is on sale

compare (kuhm-PAIR) to look closely at two or more things to see how they are different and alike

Food shopping doesn't have to be such a chore. With a little planning and some tips, you can become a smart shopper.

You woke up hungry this morning. You went into your kitchen and opened the refrigerator. There were only three lonely items. There was a half-empty jar of peanut butter. There was a carton of milk that smelled bad. There was also an apple. That's hardly enough to have a healthy breakfast.

There was no getting around it. You couldn't put it off anymore. It was time to go food shopping again.

Many people put off shopping because it's too confusing. There's so much to choose from. Everything seems to cost a lot of money. It seems to take hours to get from one end of the store to the other!

Shopping doesn't have to be that way. It's not that hard to become a smart shopper. It means planning what you'll be eating. It means saving and using **coupons**. It means buying sale items. It means checking the price of different brands of food.

Smart shoppers do these things all the time. Often they come away with many different healthy foods. They save money at the same time.

1. Why don't some people like shopping?

2. Name one thing that a smart shopper does.

The first tip on being a smart shopper is to plan ahead. That means making a list before you leave the house. Write down what foods you need to buy. Try to plan meals three or four days ahead. Check the kitchen for things you're running low on. Write these things on the list.

Then check the rest of your home. You'll need to buy things other than food. You may need more soap, tissues, or paper towels. Put these things on your list, too.

Then get your supermarket's **circular**. This is a paper stores print every week. You can find it in the newspaper or in the front of the store. Sometimes it may be delivered to your house with the mail. The circular tells which items are on sale that week. Look closely for the things you usually buy. Then add any sale items you need to your list.

Do one more thing before you leave for the store. Get your coupons. You can clip coupons from the newspaper and save them. Coupons are a very good way to save money. They can save you from 25 cents to more than a dollar on an item. Some coupons offer a "buy one, get one free" deal. Note on your list which items you have coupons for. Now you are ready to go shopping.

There are two goals to meet at the store. One is to buy everything you need. The list will help you do that. The other goal is to save as much money as you can.

There are five ways to save money at the supermarket. The first way is to use as many coupons as you can. As you go through the store, watch for items for which you have coupons.

The second way to save money is to buy as many items on sale as you can. Suppose you like one brand of ice cream. The store might be having a sale on another brand. Try that other brand. You'll save money, and you might even like it better.

The third way to save money is to **compare** prices of different brands of an item. For example, if there are five brands of soap, think about buying the kind that costs the least.

The fourth way to save money is to compare prices of different sized items. This can be a little tricky. Here's how it works.

Most grocery items come in different sizes. Tuna is a good example. Tuna comes in a 6-ounce can. It also comes in a 12-ounce can. The second size is twice as large as the first. But the 12-ounce size may *not* cost twice as much as the 6-ounce size. This is because all stores want you to buy larger sized items. They make more money that way. They get you to buy the larger size by giving you more for your money on larger items.

Let's say the 6-ounce can of tuna costs $1.20. That's 20 cents an ounce. The 12-ounce can costs $1.80. That's 15 cents an ounce.

The larger can is a better buy because you're paying 5 cents *less* for each ounce of tuna. The price for each ounce is easy to find because most stores display the per ounce cost right next to the price of the item.

Check the shelves to compare sizes and prices. Sometimes you don't save money when you buy the larger size. Sometimes the savings are very small.

Here's the fifth and last tip: Try not to buy things you don't need. Supermarket workers are great at making things look like you must have them! They put delicious things where you can't help seeing them. At the checkout counter, there are more items they're hoping you'll buy. Stick to your list. You'll save money.

Now you have some tips on being a smart shopper. Plan ahead and make a list. Read the store's circular and buy sale items. Clip and use coupons. Compare prices of different brands. Compare prices of different sizes. Stick to your list to save money. Follow these tips, and your next trip to the supermarket may be more interesting. It may also be cheaper!

3. Why is making a list before you go shopping so important?

4. Why does a smart shopper use the store's circular?

5. How does a coupon save you money?

6. Tell how to compare the prices of different sized items.

7. Should you always buy the larger item? Why or why not?

Breakfast

WORDS TO KNOW

protein (PROH-teen) a thing found in some foods that helps build and fix the body

carbohydrates (kahr-boh-HEYE-draytz) things found in some foods that give the body energy

cholesterol (kuh-LEHS-tuh-rohl) a soft, fat-like thing found in some foods

fiber (FEYE-buhr) a thing found in some foods that helps protect against disease

Breakfast is the best way to start the day. So don't leave home without it!

Has this ever happened to you? You're having a big test at school. You were up late the night before studying. The morning of the test, you woke up late. You had just enough time to make it to school. So you decided to skip breakfast.

Later that morning, you're taking the test. Suddenly your brain begins to slow down. You were sure you knew most of the answers. But now, many of the questions seem hard. You can't figure out what's wrong.

Your problem might have nothing to do with the test. Maybe the problem was something you did at home. Maybe it was something you *didn't* do. You didn't eat a good breakfast.

It's a fact. People who eat breakfast regularly do better at school and work than those who don't. People who eat breakfast are healthier than those who don't.

Of course, many people still find excuses to skip breakfast. It's easy. Here are three common ones: (1) I don't have the time.

(2) I'm trying to lose weight. (3) I'm not hungry early in the morning.

Those excuses are not very good reasons for skipping breakfast. Suppose you are in a hurry in the morning. You should eat something you don't have to cook. A muffin, cereal, or piece of bread and cheese takes little time to prepare. Drinking a glass of juice or eating a piece of fruit takes only a few seconds. Fixing a healthy breakfast can take less time than combing your hair.

If you're trying to lose weight, skipping breakfast is a *big* mistake. You will be tired by mid-morning. You'll be hungry. Then you'll want to eat a snack that isn't healthy. Your body will have the energy it needs only if you eat breakfast.

What if you just don't feel hungry in the morning? Put off eating breakfast. Take a morning walk or run around the block. Get dressed. By the time you are done, you may be hungry. If you still are not hungry, put breakfast in a bag and take it with you!

1. How does eating breakfast help you?

2. What is one excuse not to eat breakfast?

3. Why isn't skipping breakfast good for someone who's trying to lose weight?

Of course, eating just any food for breakfast isn't the key to good health. Too many doughnuts or sweetened cereals are bad for you. You should eat healthy foods instead. A good breakfast is made up of foods that have different things your body needs.

The first thing needed is **protein**. The body uses protein to grow and fix itself. Protein helps keep the body strong. **Carbohydrates** are also needed. These provide a lot of energy. You need a small amount of fat. Fat provides energy, too. It also keeps you from getting hungry again too soon. But too much fat in your diet can make you gain weight.

There are certain breakfast foods that can provide you with many of the things you need.

Eggs are a great source of protein. They also provide carbohydrates and fats. Some doctors have warned against eating too many eggs. Eggs are high in **cholesterol**. Cholesterol is a type of fat. Too much of this fat is unhealthy. For most people, it is healthy to have eggs only once or twice a week.

Another good breakfast food is cereal. The right kinds of cereal are those that have a lot of **fiber**. Fiber is important for good health. It protects your body against dangerous fats. It helps cut down the chances of having heart disease. Cereal should not have too much sugar, though.

If you can't eat eggs or cereal in the morning, try some fruit. A piece of fruit is a great way to start the day. Apples, oranges, and grapefruit are three good choices. All have lots of vitamins and minerals.

These are just a few ideas for healthy breakfasts. Of course, there are many, many more. You don't even have to stick to "breakfast foods" either. Other foods can make good breakfasts as well. Try tuna, chicken, or egg salad on toast, for example. Try cottage cheese and fresh fruit.

Some people say breakfast is the most important meal of the day. That may or may not be true. One thing is true, though. People who eat breakfast do better at work, school, and play. That's because all those people are starting the day the right way. They are starting with a good breakfast.

4. What things does your body get from eggs?

5. What does your body get from cereal?

6. Why should you eat different kinds of foods?

7. Why do you think breakfast is so important?

Aerobic Exercise

Most people want to be strong and full of energy. They want to look good, too. People who **exercise** can be all these things. Working out is good for you in more ways than one.

It happened again this morning. Shawna was late. She had to run for the school bus. She just made it. By the time she reached the bus stop, she was completely out of breath. The stop was only two blocks from her house!

Shawna can't understand it. She thinks she's in pretty good shape. She watches what she eats. She goes to gym class at school. Sometimes she goes skating on weekends. Still, Shawna is out of breath when she runs for a few minutes.

Maybe Shawna is not in the best shape she can be in. To be in the best shape, Shawna should exercise regularly. If she wants to look and feel great, exercising is the best thing she can do.

To feel her best, Shawna should do aerobic exercise. Aerobic exercise works the heart. As you exercise, your muscles use oxygen. The harder you work them, the more oxygen they use. That makes your heart beat faster. It has to pump more blood, which carries oxygen to your muscles. After a while, your muscles become stronger. Your heart, which is a muscle, also becomes stronger.

Aerobic exercise means steady movement. You should continue without stopping for at least 15 minutes. Jogging, bicycling, and jumping rope are good aerobic exercises. There are others, too. Swimming, walking, dancing, and skating are also good.

After a few weeks of regular aerobic exercise, you will be stronger. Your heart won't have to work so hard to pump blood. Your muscles will need less oxygen. You won't be out of breath if you have to run a couple of blocks. You will feel great!

1. What must your heart do when you exercise?

2. What do jogging, swimming, and skating have in common?

You can check if you are really doing aerobic exercise. One way is to count your heart rate. Try this. First take your resting **pulse**. Get a watch with a second hand. Sit quietly for a few minutes. Put your fingertips on the inside of your wrist. Count the beats for one minute. That pulse is your heart rate when you aren't doing something active. Most people get 60, 70, 80, or 90 beats a minute.

Now choose a form of aerobic exercise that you like. Warm up by stretching for a few minutes. Then exercise for about 15 minutes. Now take your pulse again. Your heart rate should have gone up. It should now be between 130 and 160 beats a minute. If it is, then you are making your heart and muscles stronger.

Aerobic exercise can also help you lose weight. Maybe you've been having too many cheeseburgers and milkshakes lately. It might be a good idea to start doing regular aerobic exercise. That will improve the way your body burns up fat and other foods you eat. Soon, those extra pounds will begin to drop off. You will soon look better. You'll feel better as well.

You may be surprised to learn that aerobic exercise can also help your **mental health**.

Suppose you're feeling a lot of **stress**. You are often anxious and tense. Try some exercise. You may feel more relaxed.

Perhaps you hate to exercise. Aerobic exercise isn't the only thing you can do. Many sports are also good for you.

There are team sports such as baseball, basketball, and football. Soccer and volleyball are good exercise, too. There are other sports such as tennis, skiing, and weight lifting. Some sports involve a lot of starting and stopping. They won't get your heart rate up quite as fast as steady exercise. Still, they are useful in improving your health.

People of all ages should exercise regularly. Of course, exercise alone will not keep you in good health. You have to eat the right foods. You have to get the proper amount of rest. You have to stay away from harmful things such as drugs, alcohol, and tobacco.

The healthiest people are the ones who take the best care of their bodies. If you are already one of those people, good for you. If you aren't, there's no time like the present to start. Try to exercise today!

3. How can you tell if your exercise is aerobic?

4. Name two ways aerobic exercise helps your body.

5. What is the difference between aerobic exercise and sports like weight lifting?

6. Why is aerobic exercise alone not enough to make you healthy?

7. What is your favorite aerobic exercise? Why?

Calling for Help

WORDS TO KNOW

emergency (ee-MER-jehn-see) something that needs action right away

operator (AHP-uh-rayt-uhr) the person who answers a call to 911

poison (POYZ-uhn) something that causes harm or death

hotlines (HAHT-leyenz) special phone numbers to call for help with certain things

An **emergency** can be pretty scary. You may not know what to do. But someone knows what to do to help.

A fire breaks out! The fire department is called. No one had to look up the number. The person who saw the fire break out just dialed 911 and told the **operator** who answered that a house was on fire. Soon the fire engines were on their way.

Some places don't have 911. But many places do. Thousands of people all over the country call 911 every day. There are three kinds of emergencies that 911 operators can help with. They can send police, fire, or medical help right away to those in need.

Some 911 emergencies are for the police. For example, you may see a crime. A family may come home to find their house has been broken into. In both cases, the police are needed quickly. That's a reason to call 911.

If a fire starts, that's also a reason to call 911. Sometimes a small fire can be put out. If a fire looks as if it can spread, don't take a chance. Call 911.

A medical emergency might also mean a call to 911. Suppose you or someone you're with becomes very ill. Sometimes it's not easy to tell how sick a person is. There are a few things to look for.

If a person is in very bad pain and can't move, that's an emergency. A person who passes out and doesn't wake up quickly also needs help fast. Those would be two reasons to call 911. Here is a way to help you decide. You should call 911 if you think a person should go to a hospital.

1. For which three kinds of emergencies should you call 911?

2. Name one reason you would call 911 for medical help.

Sometimes people call 911 when they shouldn't. Some people call 911 to reach the police or fire department even when it's not an emergency. For example, you might want information about parking rules. You might want to find out if you can burn leaves in your backyard. If you need to talk to the police or fire department about something that doesn't need fast action, use their regular number. Save 911 for "life and death" situations. Call 911 only when you need help right away or when someone may get hurt or die.

There are other emergencies that don't need a call to 911. For example, the electric power may go off at your house. Unless it's caused by a fire, you should not call 911. Call the local power company and tell them you've lost power. They'll tell you what's wrong. They'll even tell you when they expect to have it fixed.

Someone might swallow something that is a **poison**. You should call the Poison Control Center. Its number is in the front of your phone book. Someone will tell you quickly if what was swallowed, touched, or breathed is harmful. They will tell you what to do to help the person who was poisoned.

Sometimes you or someone you love may have a personal problem. Problems with family, friends, drugs, or alcohol may be very upsetting. Someone may be sad all the time.

People with serious personal problems may need help quickly. But 911 is not the right number to call.

Most places have special numbers to call for personal problems. These numbers are called **hotlines**. Some hotlines are for alcohol or drug problems. You can call them for help and advice. Others are hotlines for people who may harm themselves. You can call a suicide hotline if someone you know is in danger of killing himself or herself.

Most hotlines can be called 24 hours a day. The people who answer the phone know a lot. They are kind and helpful. They will talk to someone with a problem for as long as necessary.

The phone numbers for hotlines are different in each city. You can find them easily, though. Look in the front of your phone book. You will probably find these numbers on the first few pages.

Sometimes you may have a problem for which you need help. It's useful to know whom to call. There are other helpful groups listed in the phone book. Spend some time looking for them. You never know when you might need to call one.

When there is a real life-and-death emergency, think of the most important phone number of all. When you need help fast, 911 is the number to call.

3. Why should you call 911 only for a very serious emergency?

4. Give an example of an emergency for which you would not call 911.

5. Why do you think hotlines are listed at the front of the phone book?

6. Why is it important to call the right place for help?